The Dust Collector

E. M. McConnell

This book is dedicated to those who love a good
morally grey character.
If you like emotionally complex, good human people
who do heinous things, this is the story for you and it
is yours.
Greetings, my complex ones.
I see you.

Other Works by the Author
  The Sovereigns Series
  The Sunset Sovereign
  Woestynn Chronicles
  King of the Mines
  The Guard of Woesytnn
  Pilgrim

Contents

Darius

The storm was rising again. Darius pulled up his wrap, tucking it in closely around his nose. The storm looked like the normal wind but he wasn't taking any precautions, not after watching Jen die last month, his skin flaking into the air. They might not have put anything poisonous in the wind since that day but the Flames were unpredictable. If you wanted to survive, it was best to be cautious.

The wind picked up, swirling brown dust in clouds, tiny raging tornadoes that ripped and scoured the surface. He paid them no heed. The ore spots in this area were sparse, with only a few spots left on the surface – hardly worth scrabbling around for. Prisoners normally left the place alone as a result, preferring the easier pickings elsewhere. It was precisely why he had chosen to settle here when he first arrived in Woestynn.

The wind swept away, moving off towards the deserted mines, leaving the place quiet. He looked towards the mountains, shielding his eyes from the glaring Sun rising in the East. It still looked empty, the vast plains free of movement. It was time to move before the Sun got too high.

Adjusting his pack, Darius reached out to take his staff from its spot against the wall of the hut. He refused to call it home, despite it being where he had lived for longer than he wanted to imagine. It wasn't home, here. It was somewhere you had to live, or endured, until you were released or died. Home had heart in it. Hope. This place had neither.

Stepping out with a determined stride, he found his rhythm. One, two, one, two. It was almost as if he was back in the military again, marching with his fellow soldiers. Except back then, he had a life to live, a purpose.

The plains loomed on his left, great flat desert that seemed to stretch for leagues. He avoided it, keeping to the cool shade of the rocks, walking in shadow. It was quicker to cross the plains directly but the Sun beating down was torturous. It was easier and safer to take the long way, at least in the daytime. But he didn't much care for travelling at night. Not with the damned Crawlers coming out when the Sun went down.

The ground was cracked in places, creating narrow crevices of glassy rock. Darius stepped carefully, despite having walked this way countless times. The way to survive this planet was to always respect it, to never assume that you knew its secrets. He mentally catalogued his surroundings as he walked. Tower Rocks was up ahead. The great pillars of stone were stacked upon each other, almost haphazardly, as if a small child had built towers with their bare hands.

He could see the prison far in the distance, its domed humps distinct under the sun. And behind that was the Cairns, as he called it, the jagged teeth of the red mountains reaching up to the dusty orange sky. It was all so familiar to him now, more real than his old life on Mourn. He could only get snatches now of his home planet, of the fir trees waving in the wind, of the cool grey sky.

"Better that way," he murmured. "Mourn is gone. This is where you are. Focus on that, Dar."

He focused. He turned his head, wincing at the angry glare of the sun across the desert, mentally preparing himself for the searing heat later. He breathed out, his eyes logging the distance, planning out his stops.

If he got the timing right he could cover the distance, collect enough ore to pick up his weekly supplies and put something aside. What he put aside the ore for, he did not know sometimes, but it was helpful to have spare for the times of need, for if new metals came in that he could use to reinforce his shelter. Or if he needed some salve or another small necessity.

The guards were familiar with him now, and treated him almost with a geniality. Darius wondered who would be on today, cycling through names, thinking about who was there last.

He growled, shaking the thought off. What was it to him if a certain guard was on? They would not cheat him as they needed the ore, and despite all their best efforts with the winds, they had not managed to wipe out those who flocked to the Mines. They could not send civilians out to collect the ore, and it was still in demand in the wider solar system. He did not know why, and he did not care why. Let them do whatever they wanted. It did not affect him.

Rocks loomed overhead, sharp talons of shadow stretching over the sand. He hugged the rock, feeling the relief of the shade even this early in the morning. It did not matter how long you had been Woestynn's slave, you did not ever get used to her heat. She would boil those dry who did not learn. Darius was a fast learner. But still he gasped, feeling the sweat drip from his forehead, those beads of moisture that had escaped his headscarf. The heat shrivelled you somehow, beating on your forehead, on your arms, making you submit. Making you fall. She was a stern taskmistress.

But then, weren't they all. Nobody came to Woestynn for love, or because they were in need of solace. Woestynn was a planet designed to break you.

He pushed on, his eyes lowered as the sun rose, unfurling her ferocity, the heat beating on his forehead, his skin. He felt the heat branding him, hearing the pulsing rage of the huge Sun as it blazed down. Had it not branded him enough already? He felt the pulsating burn spread as he strode, even in the shadow. He wished for the wind, dry and hot as it was, to lift some of the heat away.

Look at me, the sun commanded. He did not look up. To look up into that heat was death, a searing of the eyes that blinded the hopeful prisoner. Never look up.

His instruction, to so many new prisoners, resounded in his mind. It warred with the part that wished to end it, to look up, to stop this purgatory. The new prisoners did not always listen either. He couldn't blame them. Their end was not short but was still more merciful.

It did not matter though, to him. The Sun may call so sweetly but his crime was not one that would invite a speedy purgatory. As if they could purge their crimes so easily. They were caught in Woestynn not to find forgiveness, but to face death, slowly, to see it flaying blistered skin, burned faces, before ripping their minds away from its wretched consciousness. And that was if they were lucky.

He tore his mind away from that, from his objective. Find ore, collect funds, and go back to your shelter. That is why you are here.

He gripped his staff, concentrating on the feel of it, putting one foot carefully in front of the other.

One, two, one, two.

The rocks continued to provide him with some shade, although he was careful not to touch the rock, now. As the sun rose she heated the rocks up almost to boiling point. When the stones began to gleam and shine, that was when they were too hot. He had seen one explode once, shattering into sharp shards like knives, slicing into the air. A beautiful, deadly sight. He still had some of the pieces, the sharp ones, stowed away in his pack. They were useful for starting fires and for defending himself if the Crawlers got too near.

The wind picked up a little, moving back over the plains. Darius adjusted the pack, then pulled his scarf up a little. He was thirsty, his mouth and throat dry. But that was normal. The agonising burn of thirst was an ever present companion in the day. He thought longingly of the hydration tablets that rested in the bottom of his bag. The thing that kept him alive. One, two. One, two. Keep walking, he thought. Hydrate when you get to the ore field. Keep going.

The rocks to his right began to change, the sharp shapes giving way to the glassier, smoothed shapes of volcanic rock. He climbed, stepping onto the flat surface, walking through the corridors of rock, hearing the echo of his boots. It was cooler here, sheltered by the rocks, and he welcomed the respite, brief though it was. He stepped out on the other side, feeling the sun greet him again with a wall of heat. It burned his eyes, slamming them with heat, drying them out again. He looked down, searching for which spots had been exposed by the winds since yesterday. The winds had been busy. There were patches here and there of exposed ore, dark brittle black gleaming strong against the burnt orange sand. He unhooked his pack from his shoulders, setting it on the ground, as he rolled his shoulders. He should be able to collect enough today for a reasonable amount of supplies.

Opening his pack, he removed his tools, the pick and the shovel. Despite all the technology that civilisation had, nobody had improved on the simplest tools to mine with, either above or below ground. Or if they had, they did not give them to prisoners like him.

Bent double, Darius scraped, lifted and removed the ore, painstakingly placing it into his backpack. He worked efficiently, ignoring the strain in his back from bending. He would work that ache out on the walk to pick up supplies. Life here was never without pain. His pack was full at last, and there was much ore still remaining.

Wiping the sweat from his brow, Darius undid and retied his headscarf, tucking it firmly around his chin. He scooted back against the rocks, finding a spot where the sun could not peep in. He rested his head against the rocks for a moment, letting the fatigue leave his body. He pulled the pack closer, fingers searching for the hydration tabs.

He had a good supply, but he still rationed himself carefully. He did not want to experience the hot sun without them to hand. He found one, wrapped in the foil to keep them fresh. Deftly, he unwrapped it and threw it into his mouth, shutting his eyes as the tablet dissolved quickly, sending moisture into his mouth and down his throat. His lips were still cracked, dry. But there was no point in changing that yet, not till the sun lowered over the horizon and he was back at the shelter.

Stretching his legs out, he almost found a moment of peace, sitting there in a crevice in the rocks. He rested his head again, shutting his eyes. He could afford a few moments before he began the walk to the dispensary.

Not for the first time he wished he could smoke, to pack a pipe full of tobacco and draw it in slowly, enjoying the pull of the smoke, the quiet contemplation. But there was none to be had here, and in any case, it would dry his throat even more. He had not tasted tobacco in years, but he still missed it.

Time passed, slowly. He may have dozed a little, eyes closed, sheltered in the rocks. But then he stirred himself, readying for the long walk. He shouldered the pack carefully, rocking a little from the weight as he adjusted. He picked up his staff again, stepping back out into the hot desert sun. This time he walked towards the plain, heading for the road that marched straight to the prison. There was no other way to the prison, at least, not in this part of the desert.

He could see the prison structure ahead of him, the black buildings crouching in the sand. It was empty, the desert, which surprised him. He would have expected to see a few figures doing the same as him, dropping off ore. Not that he often spoke to them. There was no point in making allies here, of the other prisoners. Either they were in thrall to the Mine King, or they were hanging on to the hope that they could get into the prison someday, clutching up ore to present to the Warden in a pitiful attempt at redressing the wrongdoings, the sins, that they had committed. He understood it, of course. Hope is a dangerous thing.

The pack was heavy. Very heavy. He would be glad to rid himself of it, of the sharp pieces that dug into his back, making him wince. The buildings grew nearer, and the road widened slightly. At least the road was well maintained, fairly free of dust and debris. His feet crunched on the surface, a staccato tap of progress.

One, two, one, two.

He could make out the low building of the Dispensary, see the open door, the counter within. Not far now.

There were two guards inside, both tall, with cropped hair and weapons strapped to their backs. But they were relaxed, talking to each other, leaning against the counter as if they had been propping up a bar back home after a day in the mines. The first one turned, alert, and then nodded briefly to Darius as he approached. "Proceed, Inmate."

Darius bowed his head respectfully. It would not do any good to antagonise them. He stepped up to the counter, taking his bag gratefully from his shoulders and removing the contents, spreading it out on the counter.

The guards pulled out the scales, the scanners and the parts to store the ore in. They were used to this game. Wilkes, the taller one, got paper out and started to take notes, quickly. "You got some good specimens today, Darius," he said. "Do you want to put any aside to pay off your freedom?"

Darius shook his head. The guard eyed him then shrugged. "Not one for talking today, are you. Alright then. What supplies will you be needing? You've got enough for the usual and I can throw in a bit extra.

We've got no new stuff in yet, we're expecting a transportation to arrive soon, but there's been some delays. Something or other to do with the strikes, I reckon."

The other guard, Kramer, finished his measuring and said something quietly to Wilkes. Wilkes nodded to him. "The devils have been on the move the last few days, Darius. You might want to keep an extra eye out, make sure they don't take you. We don't want to lose our best Collector to their depraved hands, do we? You'd be safer inside the cells, you know. Perhaps you should think about it."

Darius shook his head again. "Just the supplies, please, Sir. And thanks, for the tip."

His voice sounded rusty with disuse, paper thin. But Wilkes didn't seem to notice. From behind him an automaton whirred, whisking about collecting the supplies that Darius needed. The pile grew, as the automaton added packets of powdered food and the hydration tablets. His eyes fell on the pile of blankets and new boots, no doubt waiting for the new intake of prisoners due with the transport. He considered whether to purchase new boots or not, or wait and see if he could scavenge some later. There were always new boots to be had when the crawlers had made off with the new prisoners. It seemed wasteful to buy a pair.

The Guard followed his eyes and looked at the stacks of blankets and clothes.

"You'll be crowded out there soon, Darius. We have around a hundred new prisoners being transferred from Kronak. It could get busy. If you know what I mean."

Darius knew what he meant. The guards would fire up the winds to corral the prisoners, keeping the crawlers away from the prison. But they were still snatched, carried off to the Mines to serve the King. Or they died, their skin stripped by the feral mouths of the prisoners who lived in the sand. He nodded.

The automaton had finished, bringing up the supplies to the counter. Wilkes took the parcel, stowing it into Darius' pack. He leaned, reaching under the counter, and took two more items which he placed on top before closing the pack, pushing it towards him.

"I put a couple of comforts in for you, Darius. As a bonus. Same time next week?"

Darius nodded. "Yes, Sir. Thank you."

The guards returned to their conversation as he stepped out, shouldering the pack again. It was heavy, but this time the pack was smooth in its bulk, packed full of the supplies he needed. He turned his face towards the shelter, mentally counting the steps.

One, two, one, two.

Back to the shelter, refuel and rest. Tomorrow would be a new day.

Making Friends

The hut welcomed him, looming up all of a sudden in the desert, looking just as it always did. A small sigh of relief escaped his lips as he approached , seeing the lack of life. He did not want the Crawlers to discover the place where he stayed, to rifle through it, to lie in wait for his return. It was unlikely that prisoners would venture here but sometimes they did. Solitude carried its own pain but coming into contact with the Crawlers was something else entirely. He would live entirely without human contact before meeting one of those again. He shuddered.

Placing his staff against the doorjamb, he pushed inside, holding his pack carefully, barring the door behind him. Inside was spartan, but neat, with one high up window, there to let a little light and air in but not to see out with, unless you were looking for the stars. He had fashioned himself a bed, with blankets neatly tucked. There was a small metal table in one corner and a makeshift hearth for kindling. He rarely used it, because he was afraid of smoke rising and alerting the crawlers, but sometimes it was a comfort to create fire. He placed his pack in the corner, unravelling his headscarf and draping it on the table to air. The splash of colour from the scarf brightened up the otherwise bland hut.

He cast an eye at the waning sun, calculating how long it would be before night fell. He did have some battery for lights but he preferred to not use it if he could. Sometimes it felt more instinctual, somehow, to follow the pattern of the day. It reminded him of his own grandparents who slept as soon as the suns set over their farm.

The sun was still high, and the moon had barely cleared the horizon. He had time. He needed to hydrate and he wanted to eat, if you could count mixing a nutrition tablet with a hydration tablet eating. He did not, but it was all he had. Darius recalled the guard mentioning comforts as he put something into his pack. He wondered what he had put in, carefully removing the food packs and hydration tablets, placing them in neat piles.

As a rule the guards did not cheat him or short-exchange him, but there was always one or two. When he noticed that he would avoid that guard for a while. It always righted itself eventually.

His fingers touched something unexpected and he paused. Adjusting his position for a moment he cast a look outside again, to be sure, and then reached back in carefully to see what the guard had put in. It was a cloth, a small cloth that held something hard inside. He unwrapped the material carefully, curious. Inside was a black brick, around the size of the palm of his hand. Curiously, he lifted it to his face and inhaled. He laughed as he set it back down.

Tea. That would certainly be a difference to water, and welcome in the cold nights! He laughed again, and put it reverently to one side. He reached in again and pulled out a fresh, laundered headscarf, soft and clean. He gasped, holding it to the light. His joy was tempered by a sudden fear. Why would they help him?

He resolved to avoid that guard for a while, just in case. But he would keep the scarf. He placed both items on the table, looking at them in the dying afternoon light. He stirred, coming back to himself and painstakingly repacked his bag, adding enough hydration tablets to last a few days, one sachet of food and then burying the rest beside the hearth. It would never do to be unprepared.

A skitter of movement near the makeshift ceiling made him jump and he pushed himself back, eyes darting wildly. What was that? He stilled, waiting.

It wasn't a Crawler. Calm yourself.

His heart returned to a calmer state, yet attentive. He waited. There it was again, a glimmer of movement. This time his eyes tracked it, a small shape that ran across the wall, huddling the ceiling. A sand lizard perhaps, he thought, relaxing. They would not hurt him. They were too small to cause harm. It was probably afraid of him. He wouldn't be surprised if others out there ate them. People could be driven to desperate measures, far too easily. But he would not.

"Welcome, little fellow," he murmured. "Stay as long as you like. But don't make a nest in my bed."

He gestured to it with his hand, then laughed at his foolishness. "Talking to a lizard. Imbecile."

Scooting back so as not to disturb the little fellow, he felt his back hit the rough frame of the bed. He pulled himself up onto it, stretching out for a moment, watching the lizard. He would make food a little later. For now, he would see if the lizard wanted to make a home there. He wondered if it would perhaps stay a while. And with that, as his limbs relaxed, his eyes shut.

***

It was dark. Darius could feel it as he opened his eyes, in that quiet stillness outside the hut. He must have slept for longer than he expected. But no matter – he was not afraid of the silence. His eyes slipped to his pack, still in the position he had left it. Good.

But he listened anyway, his hand poised over the weapon jutting from the frame of the bed, his heart beating, steady, but fast. It was silent. No screams. No feet hitting the sand. He stared at the ceiling, his eyes fixed on that one point where there was an irregularity in the wood, where he had to patch it with oddments of stone, wood and cloth.

But there was no sound. His hut was safe. He breathed out, slowly. It was a hell of a thing to not even feel safe where you lived, but that was the price of Woestynn. It was why there would always be empty cells waiting for desperate prisoners who couldn't take the desert anymore. He did not blame them, not one bit. But he would never join them. That, he knew. He would live out the rest of his miserable life on his own terms, not rotting in a cage.

He released the blade, his hands moving to the wood of the frame, his legs hitting the floor with a dull thud. The fleeting shadow of his friend moved from his spot to somewhere else, startled.

"Hey now, Mister, don't be scared!"

His crooning was neither musical nor gentle, but perhaps the lizard was used to harsher climes. It did settle, its legs slowing, its head looking around again. Darius felt a moment of relief, of satisfaction. He didn't go. That was something wonderful. He wondered what lizards even ate. Could he find something to tempt him with here?

He probably did not want reconstituted powdered food. But then, he had grown up on a desert planet. Maybe he was used to dry.

He moved carefully towards his pack, taking out a couple of sachets carelessly. Looking up, he smiled.

"Dinner time, Mister. I doubt you'll want this, but I have extra. If you want to try it, I can pull up a plate!"

Mister did not approve, based on his lack of reaction. His tail curved against the frame, his eyes fixed on something else. Darius did not mind. The lizard did not need to actually interact with him at all. He had stayed. That was good enough.

Carefully, he read the instructions on both packets and then decanted one into the other, watching the steam rise. It did not matter that he had done this same thing a thousand times already. He did not want to waste food going off the path, being experimental. Staying on the established path had its merit. Perhaps they had changed the instructions. It wasn't like he was rushing somewhere anyway.

He felt the familiar crinkle as the food resettled into something like its original form, not resembling the animal it came from or even the vegetables it professed to have, but it steamed, letting off a wholesome scent. Each packet was nutritionally adequate for a grown man to function on for at least half a day, if not more. It did not replace actual meals or the actual feeling of eating, but it fulfilled their calorific needs.

Darius picked up the eating utensils, pushing inside and scooping out a mouthful, not thinking about how it looked, how it would taste. It was fuel. No more. When he first arrived he would carry on imaginary conversations with his ma, even re-enact Feast Days for her entertainment. But she became stale, repetitive, as he scrabbled for new material to populate her with, and at last he discarded her. Not because he did not love his mother, his family. He did. But because he knew that having an imaginary conversation with her, however pleasant it was, would only last so long. People need new stimuli. And that he did not have. So rather than keep up the pretence, he let her rest.

The food was welcome. He had not broken his fast under the hot, summer sun, other than hydration tablets. He preferred to not choke down powder laden nutri-packs when out in the open. It was easier to be hungry for a while. At least you still felt something.

Mister had not moved, furling out his tail and claiming his spot.

"Hey, are you coping up there, buddy?"

Mister swept his tail. In assent, maybe.

"That's good enough for me, pal. While we live together I should tell you: I don't mind quiet, I don't mind you keeping to yourself. You be social when you like, right?"

The lizard moved, putting his head up towards what he thought was the sky.

Darius smiled. "You got it, buddy. You got it."

Pilgrim

Dawn limped in quietly, bringing cloud and what looked like it could be rain. Rain was infrequent on Woestynn, but cloud was welcome. It gave some comfort from the fierce sun and that was a blessing. Darius wasted no time collecting his pack and staff, winding his new scarf closely around his mouth and his nose. He could get out further today, do some scouting for ore spots and collect enough for the hotter days. He set out with what could amount to be a spring in his step, on another planet, in another life.

He set out East, deciding to tackle crossing the plains while the weather was merciful. He faced the mountains, their towering heights looking grey-blue in the early morning light. They looked no less forbidding. But he kept his feet towards his destination, away from the mountains, towards the areas where he had not mined or investigated in a long while. When the sun was high, crossing the desert was a sure death sentence, but today the sun was swathed in cloud.

Today was a day for new possibilities. If he moved fast he could be there and back before nightfall.

His stride was sure, the excitement fuelling his legs, as he walked, staff moving, wondering what would be out there. It was easy to settle in one place in the desert and never move on, never find somewhere more suited. What could be more suited in the desert, anyway? There were no havens here. But there were different views, and he should perhaps familiarise himself with more with this planet. The dunes began to undulate a little, stepping up and down, and he adjusted his pack, holding onto his staff.

It looked all the same out here. How far would it take to walk entirely around the planet and end up in the same place? He did not know. He expected that nobody did, not in the real sense of actually walking it. Who would risk life and limb to do it? Not the guards, but perhaps the architects and builders of the prison did. Maybe even the people who built the mines, once. Darius shivered. He could not look at the looming structures without feeling a spasm of fear. What lay in there? What made the creatures, them?

He shook his head, shaking off his worrisome thoughts, shaking off the fear. It was a day for walking, for scouting out safe places for ore. It was not a day for lingering on the dark places under the earth. He concentrated on his feet, on the rhythm, and he looked out, memorising the slight changes in terrain. The wind picked up slightly, snaking over the desert, and Darius tightened his scarf reflexively. Just in case.

The sand flowed under his feet, rolling west, it felt, as he moved steadily away from the mines. He preferred to have those out of his eyeline if possible. Here the mountains were slowing, breaking down into staggered, gentler slopes, merging into the landscape. Darius wondered how many sandstorms you saw in places like this. There was nothing to break it up, nowhere to hide. But today should be fine. He was hopeful. He aimed for the shoulder of the mountains, not wanting to be caught out in the middle of the desert, just in case the weather changed.

Glancing again at the sky, he moved off, focusing on the soft thud of the staff in the sand. It felt no less dry but he imagined that it was less yielding, stronger, enjoying the scant moisture left behind by the ruthless sun. Could a desert be sentient, and wish for moisture and cool rain? He scoffed at himself for his whimsical thoughts. It was like something his ma would have said, once. Before the sorrow stripped her laughter away. His mouth tightened. He had caused that.

The land had shifted, giving another horizon, one of flatter sand dunes against a swirling orange sky. The clouds were grey, wrapping the sun up in a stranglehold. Darius smiled grimly. It wasn't as if they needed the sun here. She was a blight on the landscape. The mines were less distinct, a little more tucked behind the mountain ranges. His heart sagged, relieved. He cast a practised eye over the dunes, frowning.

The sand here was high, pliant, furrowed in waves thanks to the wind. It did not look like a good place to mine ore. Glancing at the sun, or at least, the light behind the clouds, he tried to calculate how long he had been walking for. Normally he could do so by his thirst, but today was unusually cool. He suspected that he would not need more than one or even two hydrations. That was unusual. His legs were not especially fatigued, although today his pack was light. He would be able to walk some time yet before he needed to rest.

The dunes were difficult to walk, slipping under his feet, making his legs stagger. He would not like to be chased out here. Uneasily, he glanced towards the Mines again, far in the distance. But it was day, and the Crawlers did not usually come out in the day. But the fear still caught in his throat. He did not want to encounter them. It had been a while, and he wanted to keep it that way.

To the west of him the terrain looked firmer, with rocks anchoring the sand and foiling the soft waves of the dunes. He altered his direction, taking a look back behind him to make sure he knew where he was. He did not want to get lost on his way back. The rock shone in front of him, flashing out hints of blue. It could be volcanic rock. Perhaps the insides of the planet were as hot and dangerous as the outside.

The rock was sharp and glassy, jutting up from the sand like teeth. Darius stepped gingerly, not wanting to slice open the soles of his boots. Not only would it hurt, but the smell of blood could draw out the small predators that lived on the surface. They might not be able to kill him, but some of the furred ones had a nasty bite. It was doubtful he would survive an infection, not without being forced to pay his way into the hospital wing. And that could be a painful death. It was better to be cautious.

It was quiet. Quieter than normal, maybe, if you could call normal an absence of birds, of people. A bird wouldn't survive this place. He didn't know how the wildlife survived, either. There was very little of it. Sometimes he would see an armoured beetle scuttle into the stones, black shell winking. But usually it was empty.

Darius took a moment to catch his breath, looking out at the desert, at the landscape. The sky was a sullen orange, with the gun-metal clouds still obscuring the sun. There would be rain later, maybe. If there were vegetation, it would spring up green and alive after a downpour, but he had never seen any plants in this place. He wondered what the few animals here lived on, in their underground homes. Probably better not to know.

His eyes caught a sliver of movement on the horizon. What was that? He waited, his breath quickened, staring out. Nothing happened. This was not good. This was not good at all. Glancing back, he wondered if he should just head back, find some ore in the back of the Cairns maybe, and not come back. But what if they had already seen him, whoever it was? It was fairly flat and exposed. He might draw them back to his hut.

He pressed on, his senses alert to what could be ahead of him. His brain ran through possibilities. It wasn't Crawlers. They only came out at night, and you heard them first. It wasn't the new intake of prisoners, as they wouldn't be here so fast, even if they had already been dropped off. It could be guards, he supposed, coming back from one of the other Depositories. It could be another prisoner, but why would there be a flash? They didn't have access to anything that shone or reflected the sun.

He adjusted his pack, his face grim. He could feel sweat sliding down his back, cold lines of wet that would not stay for long. He ignored them. They were only relief till they were gone, it was easier to pretend they were not there. He walked on, his legs beginning to burn. The pack was uncomfortable, digging into his shoulders. Darius didn't take his eyes from the horizon. If there was another flash, he would see it. The ground here was firmer, packed more closely. He could walk more easily here, and his leg muscles would thank him for it.

The horizon got no nearer, but at least it wasn't shimmering with heat. The land was flat, broken up with flat and jutting out rock, with some seas of flowing sand. He stuck to the rocky areas, picking his way through, wondering what lived out here, if anything. There was no ore, but he saw no signs of life.

The mountains to his right, those sheltering the mines, were now just a smudge of blue. He was out in the plains, too far to turn back, really. He had to find out what was on the other side. The ground was still packed, solid. His feet hit the surface, boots crunching on the hard sand. It was almost like a road, a track...

He felt a jolt of awareness. Something had changed. He looked again, considering the terrain with a soldier's eye, not just a dust collecting one. This part of the sand was straight and wide, wide enough for a vehicle – but they did not have those out here. Did the prison guards use vehicles? He did not know, but he had never seen them using transports when he was near the Depository. If they had something, would they not use it?

This was not the time to get frightened. He was out in the middle of nowhere, too far from his hut.

Are you a man, or a mouse? he asked, grimly, eyes sweeping the horizon. He half fancied it sounded like Sergeant Tide, his dulcet tones ringing out with such contempt for his rabble of a team. "Hop to it, children!" he would shout. Well he was hopping to it, alright. He couldn't go back, not yet, so the only way was on.

The road, or what seemed to be a road, stretched on, cutting its way through the red desert like a thread, or a piece of material stretched out to mark the way. There was nothing on either side of him, no shelter, no cover of the mountains. The clouds were still covering the sun. That was something.

The land was rising steadily, although it still looked flat over a distance. The road was straight, well-tended, and Darius walked it with a sinking feeling. He had been living near this for months and he had not known. What else did he not know?

He would know this. If there were some kind of civilisation, he would take a look, and leave. Perhaps he needed to move, find somewhere else to settle. He could dismantle the hut fairly easily, and move it in a day or two, if pushed to do so. There were other spots that were not overrun by ... well whoever these people were. He didn't know.

The ground was firmer still here, rising more gently, and he could feel a soft breeze. It was welcome, and he breathed it in, feeling the difference between the slower air nearer the mountains. He could also feel vibrations, movements. Stilling, he threw himself down, pulling his backpack carefully to one side and moving up the hill. He looked down, amazed. The ground looked like it went on for miles here, onwards and onwards, but actually it ended abruptly, carved into a stop, dropping to a surface many feet below. Scooting closer, he drew out his hand, touching the edge of the cliff. It was hard. It must be man-made.

Darius scanned the area, logging details. He could see a sheer wall leading to the flat surface which was pitted with small holes. There were markings on the walls and some dark spots which looked like entrances. Or exits, perhaps. The vibration came from the wall itself, a rhythmic sound that corresponded with his heart, which was pounding. Perhaps they had created a new mine. Looking to his right, he searched for people. Would there be people? There must be! What was this place? He saw nothing different, just the wall, and the plain. He did not like this at all. It was time to leave.

He reached for his pack, crawling away from the edge, just in case someone happened to be looking up. He wondered if there were eyes on him already. He shivered. He would not come this way again. Turning west, he looked towards the mountains, considering a different route. He would go back and then retrace his steps back when he knew he wasn't being followed.

His mind churned. What was it there? Who owned it? Was it something to do with the prison? It could be, perhaps. If it was manmade. He could have accepted that it was abandoned, part of whatever the planet business was before it became a prison, but for the vibrations. Something was happening in there. But he was not going to investigate it.

He left the road as soon as he was able, stepping into the soft dunes with some relief. It had been a long time since he had tasted something like civilisation, and he did not like it much. He straightened his back. One, two, one, two. It would be alright.

"Greetings, stranger."

The soft voice was quiet but it held menace. Darius stilled, looking up at the clouds to regain his clarity. Adrenaline surged into his limbs, as he felt the smooth wood of his staff in his fingers. He did not know who was behind him but he was armed. He had killed before. He narrowed his eyes as he spoke.

"I was not aware that speaking to someone's back was a greeting. But you are right, I am a stranger."

He turned, slowly. There was a man in front of him, dressed in brown weathered garments. His face was smiling, his wrinkled skin puckered into lines, but the eyes were unblinking, the eyes of a predator. His hair was wild, long grey hair that blew in the gentle wind. He didn't move.

Darius waited, watching the man. He did not look armed, but he had an air of confidence about him. He also looked very well-fed. Was he from the encampment?

As if he had read his mind, the man smiled more widely. His eyes glinted.

"Perhaps we should become more acquainted, then. They call me Pilgrim. I have been here some years, I think. And you?"

Darius paused. "Perhaps a little more than a year. It is hard to tell."

Pilgrim nodded, the smile still stretching wide on his face. "Yes, it is. Woestynn does not give us the luxury of knowing how much time we have laboured, or how much time we have left. It is a hard mistress."

Darius did not recognise Pilgrim's dialect. He sounded as if he was a Southlander, but there was something flat in his inflection, in his tone. He opened his mouth to ask, then stopped. This was not a social call.

"What can I do for you, Pilgrim?"

He may as well get it out there in the open. If there were to be conflict, then he would not wait for it.

Pilgrim smiled again, but this time it was less pronounced, more real. "It is what Pilgrim can do for you, Stranger. Pray tell, what's your name? It's real nice to meet someone in these parts, you know. We should be more cordial with our fellow humans, do you not think? After all, we are in this together."

They were certainly not in this together. Darius nodded, adjusting his stance, watching Pilgrim do the same, flowing through his feet as if he was underwater. This man was a trained fighter.

"My name is Darius." He quelled the sudden urge to ask again what Pilgrim wanted. It would make him sound afraid.

Pilgrim lifted his fingers to his forehead as if he were about to salute or to lift his hat in respect. "Well it's real nice to meet you, Darius. And it's nice to see another human out here in the desert. I don't see many, well, not out on the plains."

He paused, considering, and Darius tightened his hand on his staff.

"I don't know if you come this way often, Darius, but there are a group of us who have a community just near here, over that hill. Perhaps you saw it?"

Darius raised his eyebrow but did not reply. Pilgrim chortled to himself, his eyes not moving. "Well, perhaps you were just out for a stroll. We have a community here, grown from the unfortunate men who were sent here, and it is growing well. We work hard, but we are all equal. And we have some access to the outside world, too."

He paused, as Darius turned in shock. They could contact the outside world?

Pilgrim laughed. "I thought that would get your interest, Darius, my friend. See, we are friends already. How about that."

He reached into his coat slowly, hand disappearing into a dark mass of leather. His other hand came up, palm up, in a stop gesture. "Don't be coming closer, now, friend, I'm getting something from my pocket. There's no need to get all troublesome now."

Darius relaxed his hand on the staff, but did not take his eyes from Pilgrim. This man was not what he said he was, he was sure of that. Pilgrim pulled out a circular disk, holding it between his fingers and reaching out towards him. Carefully, Darius took it, inspecting the disk. It wasn't completely circular, and was blackened on one side. There were markings but he couldn't make them out.

"Call that a gift from me, friend," Pilgrim said in a breezy fashion. "If you want to join a new community, just present that to the people who find you. They'll direct you to me."

Darius nodded his thanks, putting the disk into his shirt carefully. "And you are important in this community, Pilgrim?"

Pilgrim laughed, a harsh sound that did not inspire Darius to laugh along with him. "You could say that, friend. You could say that."

He turned, his coat flying behind him, as his hair gleamed. "I'll just be along now, Darius. If you get tired of being out there, you come and find your destiny, you hear?"

Darius did not answer, but Pilgrim did not wait. Loping off he became a figure on the landscape, a dark brown blot that moved along the sand. Darius stayed still, waiting, until he disappeared into the distance, before turning back towards his hut. He would go the long way. Just in case.

The Winds

The wind curled in, kicking up the hot red dust at his feet, swirling round his ankles. Darius flinched, hating the feel of its caress, of the touch of the ground against his legs, of the wind that pressed his clothes close to his body, so intimately.

In a world where you are never touched, a gust of wind can feel like an invasion. An attack.

It howled, plaintively. Darius tugged his scarf up, tighter, around his mouth and tried to plug his ears with it. The sound was still there but thankfully removed, somewhat, so he could finally think.

What was it about this place? Nothing was gentle here. His breath huffed out, panic trying to take over. That wouldn't do. The flying sand would clog the wet scarf and he would never be able to breathe.

Slow. Slow it down. He breathed, slower, feeling his heart racing. Slow down. Slow. It slowed. Darius loosened his fists slowly, unclenching them from their stranglehold, flexing his fingers.

"Alright then." His voice was muffled behind the scarf, his breath leaving the material damp, and stiflingly hot. His eyes flicked over the ground, looking to see if there had been any ore unearthed from the scrape of the wind.

Just to his right the sand had been blown apart, exposing dark patches in the soil. His heart leaped, as he moved towards it. The wind buffeted him, pushing him away, forcing him to push back, forcing himself into place. The muffled roar punctuated his breath.

The new ore was freshly uncovered, not yet ready to leave the surface. He would need his tools. Bringing down his pack, he pulled them out, tucking his chin further into the scarf. The wind screamed in his ears, its voice mocking.

Darius focused, cleaving the ore, putting it in his pack, looking out with dry eyes to the next patch that had been exposed. The orange winds rolled in the desert, dancing with the wind. He had not seen it like this in months. Could it be an artificial wind?

His hand instinctively went to the scarf, tugging it tighter. Just in case.

The wind changed tone, taking that hate up a notch, the shriek a little wilder. Darius's mouth dried, the inside of his mouth a desert, if that could be possible here. The fear rose. Hands feeling numb, he pulled the scarf as tight as it could go, eyes hunting for a safe spot.

It's changing, it's changing, find shelter. His brain started to scream, emitting flashes of panic.

There was a gap in the rock. It wasn't perfect but it was enough. If the Flames had sent a wind to boil the skin, he was in for a treat, but otherwise he could survive this. He set his back to the wind, pulling his pack, tucking himself into the crevice, feeling the strong stone at his back. He shut his eyes, pulling up the cloth. Blinded.

A waiting corpse. Waiting to die.

His legs trembled, giving way under him, as he shivered, waiting. The winds screamed. This was not a desert wind. Reaching out, scrambling, his fingers hunted for his pack. He needed to hide. His fingers felt the rough canvas and he pulled, throwing it in front of his face, hiding behind his flimsy shield, the cloth scratching his face.

The wind had voices in it. Yipping, screaming and howling, it buffeted against him, pushing his skin, swirling around, away, and back again. Breath came in pants, taking in as little as he could, as his heart pounded so hard he thought it would come out of his chest. Was this where he would die? Would he die here?

His hands tightened on the pack, holding it closer. The wind screamed, battering the walls, his hands. The sound, the sound, it was killing him. Hot tears fell as his face stretched into a shriek, or a shout? He did not know. He was going to die, here, huddled in the sand. The wind was his executioner, at last. The wind.

The wind burned his hands, ripping at his skin. The wind whipped up, screaming, whistling its rage. The cliffs around him shook, trembling against the force of the desert. Woestynn was mighty, but the Flames were mightier. And then, it stopped. The wind disappeared as quickly as it had arrived, leaving behind in memorial its absence, that echo of silence weighing on his ears, inside his skull.

He did not dare to move. The pack was his comfort, the cloth welded to his face. He focused on his hands, feeling the sting of the sand that had scraped them raw. He would need to get them treated fast. Slowly, he moved the pack away, pulling the cloth down to expose his eyes. The desert was quiet. Here and there the ore gleamed, polished by the toxic winds. His hands screamed, they were raw and blistered. Carefully, he fished out a cloth, wrapping one hand, and painfully putting the pack on his back. The ore could wait. Today he needed to rest.

He turned his face away from the mocking spread of ore, dark against the sand. It had nearly killed him today. And he did not know whether he was ready to die, or not.

Good at Waiting

The blood sun rose slowly, as if it was glutted with prey, with her winnings. It repelled him, this Sun, it was dark and harsh and unforgiving. But then, he was used to a younger, more mellow one, that helped forests grow and thrive. Barely anything grew here in the desert. Darius sat in the meagre shelter of the shade from his hut, looking out to the sky. The guard had warned him that company was coming, and something told him that would be today. If it was, he was not going to risk his neck by hauling himself out to collect anything today. No, it was safer to stay well away from the prison on the intake days.

Unbidden, thoughts rose of the man out there in the desert, the one who had said there was a community. Pilgrim. Should he have mentioned to him that there were new prisoners coming? Would he have cared? He didn't seem the type to be threatened by new blood. Perhaps even by Crawlers. He wondered again, and not for the last time, if it would be better to trek back over the plains, and hand in the coin, and see what Pilgrim could offer.

He rubbed his hand against his roughened cheek in thought. Enough of daydreaming. He had ore to collect, and days to fill. But what if it was going to be one of those days?

He had enough to not go today, but if the intake was actually tomorrow, he could struggle. Perhaps it would be good to collect some ore and store it, and then go tomorrow if the coast was clear. He cast his eye up again, eye squinting at the wrath of the sun, even though it was still early. Did he see something then? There was usually a flash as the transports broke through the atmosphere. Had he seen that?

Go with your gut, his daddy had always said. If in doubt, go with what your gut was saying. He was no coward, or at least, not before, but his gut was telling him, stay put today. His nerves jangled, as if there was a storm coming. There would be, he supposed, if the new intake was coming.

His eyes swept the desert in front of him, looking for differences, for signs that someone had come this far into the wilderness. Nothing had changed. But he could not switch it off, the fear. He was afraid of those who were landing, really, he acknowledged. The ones who were coming.

A sequence of images ran through his mind, unbidden. The inside of the ship, gleaming, with rows of dour inmates looking at a polished floor, and the guards, armed to the teeth but wearing black hoods so they could not be identified. What did it matter if they were? Nobody there could overpower them. There was no communication with the outside. There was no way to tell anyone. It's not like they were threatened with their power.

He shook his head. He remembered the first moment stepping out into the desert, the guards handing out the packs, being told to find somewhere to hide. Him, the one who had never needed to be afraid. He had learned fear, that was true. Now he was wary of everything.

Darius shook his head, breathing heavily. He blinked, too rapidly, and shook his head again. He could feel cold sweat trickling down the back of his head. No, the shipments would come today. He would stay here, and avoid it all. Tomorrow was a new day. He stood, feeling his limbs shake, his hands quiver. He ignored it. Turning, he stepped back into the hut, considering if he should barricade the door.

"Your nerves are shot, Recruit! Pull yourself together."

His imitation of the Sergeant was atrocious but it calmed him some. All he had to do was stay away. There was nothing he could do for those who tried to storm the prison anyway. Or for those who found the Mines. What was he, a philanthropic centre? He was here to survive, You like everyone else. He looked up, hoping that Mister was still there. He was, but in a new spot tucked between two beams that held the roof up. Darius reached up, stroking his skin gently.

"We're going to have a day in today, Mister. Just do your thing. Alright?"

That seemed to be fine by Mister, so it was fine by Darius. He laid himself out on his bed, looking up at the ceiling. Sleep now, before the screaming starts? Sleep now. Always sleep now. He closed his eyes, ever obediently. And Mister followed suit.

***

Dusk rolled in with malevolence. He could feel the charge in the air, the waiting. Waking with a start, Darius listened, wondering if he should check outside. Should he go outside? He stepped to the door, opening it slightly. There indeed were the transports, lifting back up into the sunburnt sky, turning to leave the planet.

Somewhere out there, there were two hundred new prisoners about to face Woestynn. He shuddered. It wasn't the first day that haunted him, although that was indeed terrifying. It was the screaming, the sound that hung in the air for hours after, that made tears rip from his eyes and sweat pool under his arms. It got under your skin, and it stayed there. It was fear itself.

Two hundred prisoners, all people who had committed terrible crimes, facing the worst night of their lives. Would any wish that they had faced the guillotine instead? Possibly. Darius knew that he had wished for it, many times, waiting for transport, watching the black ships leaving him behind on this planet, and being alone in the dark. Sometimes death is a kindness. Woestynn was not known for being kind.

He shivered again, stepping back inside the hut, placing the beams across the door from the inside, wrapping the small window in cloth. It was doubtful that any new prisoner would make it this far on only one night, and the crawlers had their sport elsewhere, but he was not taking any chances. His hands were shaking again, tiny tremors that would not stop. He cursed, quietly, to himself. Now was not the time to fall apart. Blinking rapidly, he remembered his breathing. One, two, one, two.

Picking up his pack, he reached in, taking out the treasure that the guard had given him, the pack of tea. He would have tea, and try and relax a little. He wasn't going anywhere, after all. He put the ingredients out, methodically. Take your time. His hands were still shaking.

"Stop that," he whispered. "Concentrate. Mister, do you want to try some tea?"

Mister did not respond. Darius found his cup, a battered tin effort that had probably been a relic from the guards way back when before they upgraded. He didn't care. It was something to drink from and sometimes that helped. The hydration system was efficient but it was not satisfying. It did not rejuvenate.

The tea was damp between his fingers, a sensation that his skin was not used to. He found himself lingering over it, feeling the leaves roll under his fingers, feeling the moisture. With a shake of his head he threw the requisite pinch in, carefully wrapping up the block and stowing it away. Now for the alchemy. Two tablets were waiting, still wrapped, to be added. He picked up one, peeling and throwing it in the cup, hearing the froth and fizz. He peeled the next, carefully putting the wrapping on one side and threw it in, listening to the sound of the tea brewing. It was not like it was at home, it was not hot, but it was something. It would help. Three minutes.

He had three minutes to wait. The tension collected in his knees, his hands, the back of his head. The waiting battered down on him. Finding a spot on the floor he began his drills, following the training his sergeant had taught him years before. His muscles ached. He was an old goat now, too weary for this kind of nonsense. But he continued, stretching and pushing and moving his muscles, counting down in his head. What else was there but waiting, here? He was good at it.

One minute to go. The last one stretched into eternity, the one that never ended, the one that brought the most clarity. He stretched out, arms screaming, head down, waiting. The last minute. The seconds thudded by, punctuated by his heart-beat. His hateful heartbeat. How many beats did it have left? How long would he hear it, thudding away, marking out his time?

He shrugged the thought away. There was a time and a place for thinking, and you had to limit it before it ate you up. This was reality, and there was no changing it.

The tea was ready. He could see the fizz abating, the dark leaves leaving the surface, sinking to the bottom. Civilised people strained them, removing the leaves but Darius didn't care. He drank the water and ate the leaves. It was a different texture from the food they had and therefore was welcome. Maybe it was even healthy. Who knows.

He arranged himself comfortably, reaching slowly for the tea. It was not hot, and it was not in compa-ny. But it was enough. Strangely, he actually meant that. Even being there, alone in a hut, waiting for the nightmare to begin, this moment was enough.

"Saints Blessings to you, Mother, Father," he whispered, words tumbling from his mouth awkwardly. "Let them keep you safe."

His hands closed around the cup, holding it carefully. He focused on his movements, on lifting the cup, the drinking, the setting down. It was important to be mindful, it focused you and sent the fears away. Or that's what they said, anyway, but it wasn't true. It only kept them at arms length. It was enough. It had to be enough.

Our of the corner of his eye the Moon skittered across the sky, catching his attention, as the clouds staggered, moving awkwardly. His blood ran cold. If the moon was rising then so were they.

His eyes shut, involuntarily, his terror welding them closed. Behind his eyes he watched the shapes burrowing through the sand, coming for the prisoner in the middle, ripping him apart as if he was a piece of soft bread. He witnessed the wind scorching them, their bulging eyes staring, their faces contorted in screams. Acid rose in his throat as the tea threatened to eject itself. He put one hand onto the floor of the hut, carefully splaying his fingers. He put the other hand down. Slowly. His face felt frozen. He was frozen in place.

He listened, his hands rooted to the floor. He fancied he could hear shouts, carrying across the plain. No. It wasn't possible. He was too far from the prison. He would not hear the prisoners. But another sound slithered into his ears, caressing his soul and freezing his blood. The Crawlers.

He could hear the screaming, the undulating sound as one began and another joined, creating a deadly harmony. Darius hated that sound. He felt his eyes begin to burn, his face get hot, his hands shiver. It was so loud. The noise climbed into his brain and lodged itself there, the scream rushing from one side of his head to the other. The Crawlers. His breathing sped up. The Crawlers. The screaming. It was so loud.

Darius pushed into the ground, making his palms hurt, wishing for something to scratch him, to pierce his skin, to make him focus. Breathe. One, two, one, two. He breathed, his jaw locked. The screaming was louder, voices responding and joining, the desert echoing with their song.

"But they are not near," he whispered, his voice hoarse. "They are not coming for you."

They were not. He knew that. They preferred to attack the new prisoners, to kill and feed on one, to take others, to do with Saints knew what in the Mines. He did not want to know. At times in a fit of madness he had considered following them there, to see what they did, to see how many were there, but he could not. He faced his own chasm of cowardice, knowing that he could not get nearer to one of those monstrosities. They might have been people once, but they were not now. He did not want to go there. He did not want to become like them.

The screaming continued, the tone changing, into something more frantic, more focused. The hunt.

Darius breathed out through his mouth, pursing his lips. There was nothing but the breath. Mister moved in the rafters, his skin gleaming in the moonlight.

"It's noisy out, Mister. You don't pay it any heed, alright? Predators are hunting, but they are not after me or you. They want fresh meat. You're quite safe."

Mister turned, gazing at him from a cold black eye. Darius felt comforted.

"You and me, eh, Mister? It's us against the world. You stick with me. I'll look out for you."

He fancied that Mister nodded. He smiled, a half smile that barely lifted the corners of his mouth up, but it was something. In Woestynn, something was rare. He kept his eyes on his friend as the screaming continued, rolling across the sand in angry waves, until eventually it died away.

Three's a Crowd

Light seeped through the cloth-covered window, reaching in through the tiny gaps in the beams. A new day. It filled Darius with a new hope, as hopeless as it all was. But in the light of day, he could feel braver, perhaps. Today was a day to get supplies and replenish his ore and dust stocks. Today would be a quiet day.

He looked up, looking for Mister, hoping he would still be there. There he was, tail curled, settled between the beams. Did he need anything else to be comfortable? Would he need a nest or something similar? Darius wished he had access to the information banks that he used to have, to be able to simply place his palm on a screen and ask his question, to see the information played into his eyes or directly into his brain. He had got too used to that, to the real world. Before this.

Darius shut his eyes, focusing. It did no good to think of what was, what his life was before. This was his life now. Woestynn. The desert.

"I'll be back, Mister. Look after the place while I'm gone!"

Mister did not answer. But Darius found that it did not matter as he heaved the door shut, lifting the pack onto his shoulders. Someone was waiting for him to come back and that felt good. He felt good, almost. He adjusted the pack and looked into the still weak sun. He could do this. He could do this.

He could do this. Squaring his shoulders he turned north towards Maire's place, as he called it, even though Maire had long gone. His shelter was still there, abandoned, tucked into the cleft between the rocks, a quiet haven from the sun and the wind. It was not the most ore rich of spots but Darius knew there was enough to satisfy the Guards, who would not be that interested today in quotas and donations. They would be tired from the night before, as they always were. Sometimes they made mistakes and handed out more supplies for the ore. It was not a day to miss.

That meant that other Outsiders would come today too. And the Flames would be watching for trouble, ready to toss up their poison winds at the first sign of something brewing. As he reached the quiet shelter of craggy rocks and soft sand, he paused, retying his scarf. It did not always help, but it would keep his nose protected at least. Just in case.

His eyes cast over the sand, seeing the spots where the winds had plunged downward, driving up the sediment underneath, fracturing the desert. They assisted in that, certainly, in the mining of ore, but the prison profited, sending it to the rest of the Ruben system. Everyone needed it, or at least, those who did not rely on solar energy, the elite planets. Everyone else used it for their power. Nobody thought about those mining it or carrying it, those stuck on planets like this. Why would they? He never did either, once. Why would he?

His figure bent in the hot sun, his brow sweating, his hands burning.

Every day, this was his penance. And every day it began anew. His hands clutched and scraped at ore, collecting dust, tucking it under his arm, transferring it to his pack, in a practised motion that felt as if it was born with him now. He knew how much his pack held, and how much that would buy him today. He had accomplished this ritual so many times.

Darius looked out, his eyes straining to see into the horizon, shimmering as it was in the heat. He could leave now, drop in by the Dispensary, and pick up his supplies, then get back to Mister. Maybe he could pick up a stray branch, and do some carving this evening. He hadn't picked up a branch in a while, but perhaps it was time to do so.

His pack was barely half full. It was enough today. Scooping the last of the ore into it, he pulled it onto his back, lowering his head against the glowering sun. The Dispensary was not far. He would be there and back in no time.

His feet tramped over the burning sand, marking out a staccato beat that reverberated in his legs and back. It was all so familiar now. The landscape changed, flattening, as the prison buildings came into view, huddled into the landscape. The Dispensary was open of course, the doors gaping open, the counter empty.

He threw his pack onto it, hearing the satisfying clunk of ore, the sound of trades. He could take good things home. Home. He digested the word, turning it over in his mouth. Had he meant to say that? It was not a home. It did not matter how long he remained there for. But somehow, with Mister there, it did feel like a home of sorts.

The guard lumbered up, his face pasty, his eyes suspicious. Darius kept his eyes down. Respectful. Sometimes it did not do to be too friendly with the guards. They didn't like it. As if you were getting power over them or something. He wanted to tell them that it was hard to get power when you lived in a hut in a desert, collecting ore, and afraid of being eaten by the

Crawlers, but they would not listen anyway. And then he would get less return on his ore. He wasn't saying a thing.

"Shake it out, Inmate!"

The guard's tone was harsh, trying to be authoritarian but failing. The shake in his voice gave it away. Darius wasn't going to tell him.

Shaking out the bag, Darius stepped back, his eyes down, his body language unthreatening. He did not look but he felt the guard fish through the ore, his hands unsteady, his heart beating fast. It must have been a bad night for them too. He kept his pose casual. He would not look up. Let the Guard measure the ore and let him go.

Darius could almost hear the blood pounding in the Guard's temples, in the frenzied movements of his hands, in his breathing. Darius focused on the ground, on the slight movement of the browned grass in front of him, a small patch that seemed to have sprung up in the shade of the Dispensary. Life will always find a way.

He felt the movement of his pack being shoved back, the guard stepping back, his breath steadying. "Full rations for the prisoner!"

Darius felt the smile on the inside but he did not let it seep, not let it tug on the corners of his mouth. He knew what that meant. It meant that his meagre effort got him everything today. Their fear was his gain. He focused, keeping that beat down de-meanour, not letting them know that he had heard anything. He heard items slapping down on the counter, and he stepped back forward, his head still down, respectful.

"May I?"

He asked quietly. They could take as quickly as they gave. Who was going to side with someone like him? After what he had done?

A grunt answered him, and a hand shoved the pack in his direction. It must have been a bad night for them.

Darius caught the pack, not too deftly, and filled it without looking at what they had offered. If he won, he won. With full rations, he probably did. But there would always be another post-intake day. He had time to get back and find some wood to make Mister a house maybe, and do some carving.

He could smell the guard's sweat, his fear, as he nodded respectfully before leaving. He would need to work on that before anyone else came in. Other-wise that guard would never survive at Woestynn.

***

Muscles aching, Darius climbed the ridge, reaching the top as the sun blazed down, angry. Sweat broke out on his forehead. He did not wipe it away. Pulling the scarf forward to protect his eyes, he lowered his gaze.

The plains were quiet today. Part of him wondered where the new prisoners were, but he stifled it. It was nothing to him. They would survive or not. And if they survived then they had their sentences to serve when they got the ore together for the cell. They were not on his path.

His eyes flicked to the shadow of the Mine, far yet not far enough away. He hated it, hated the structure, the gaping black. He wished that the Flames would break it apart from within, instead of sending death winds to torment prisoners who weren't doing anything wrong. That hate ran deep, for the Crawlers. For whatever made them. For whatever drove them.

He spat, taking a better grip on his staff. Its familiar roughness reassured him. The Mine was the source of his fear, and those who lived there, but he was armed. And they did not appear in full light. He knew this, but the fear boiled in his gut, making his breath hitch, his palms sweat. The Mine loomed, leering at him. It did not matter if he looked at it, or not. It was there, the true power of Woestynn, there, in the tunnels, in the wretched dark. They all knew it, even the guards.

If you didn't know it, you ended up in there, or you ended up dead. Food, or whatever they did to you.

Blinking rapidly, he hefted the staff. Focus. He had two more great dunes to cross, moving away from the Mines in the East, and then he would be away, out of sight of them. Everything would be fine.

He crossed, striding, back straining from the pack, his staff tapping, driving into the sand. His palms burned, and his forehead dripped sweat. The Sun raged. It's what the Sun did.

One more dune. That's all he needed to clear to get near to his home, to check in with Mister, to find some peace. He needed to eradicate that panic rising, and get back to his own territory. There he would be safe. One foot in front of the other. That's all he needed to do. His feet got heavier, the pack made his shoulders ache, and his eyes burned. He was getting there.

There was someone out there. He knew it, even as his eyes searched the desert in front of him. He had seen something. His heart juddered, his breath hitched. His fingers tightened on the staff as he whirled, mouth opening in a snarl, eyes wide. What was it?

He saw nothing but sand, sand and a burnt sky. The horizon rippled in the heat. He had not imagined it. Darius waited, poised, ready to strike. What was it?

There it was again, a flash of black, something glinting in the sun. That was not a Crawler. They did not travel on their own and they rarely wore clothes. But it was something, and if it was wearing clothes, it was probably a prisoner. He braced himself for a battle. It was rare that it happened – more often than not those that lived outside avoided each other, perhaps nodding then disappearing somewhere else.

This one was new. And therefore he needed to learn what Woestynn was. Striding forward, he gripped his staff, holding it firmly between his fingers, ready to strike.

He breathed in through his nose, feeling the rush of adrenaline, the stark focus. He did not feel afraid. Reaching down, he grabbed, pulling at the person scrabbling in the sand, trying to hide. Pathetic. He threw the prisoner back, letting him crawl away, face up, fear showing in their eyes. their mouth wide and slack. This one wouldn't last. He noticed that the prisoner was young, with short hair and huge eyes. Darius towered over him, noting the fear rising in a stink from his skin.

"Who are you? Why do you follow me?"

His voice came out raspy, the anger an unfamiliar feeling. But he kept his eyes trained on the prisoner, his staff ready to connect with his soft pampered flesh.

"I, I -"

Darius shook his head. Weakness died in Woestynn. He raised his staff.

The boy's hand came up, pleading. "No, wait! Don't hurt me! I wasn't trying to follow you! I was lost, I didn't know where to go and I was so scared, Please, sir. Please don't hurt me."

He looked at the boy. It wasn't even a boy, it was breathing skin waiting to die. Why would anyone send this to Woestynn?

"Go somewhere else."

Darius turned and stepped away, lowering his staff into the ground. He could hear the rapid panting of the boy, still lying where he had put him. He sounded like a wounded animal. But it was not his problem. He walked, mentally calculating how far he would have to walk before changing direction towards his hut. He didn't want to have an unwelcome guest. Or worse, be followed by the prisoner and be scented by the Crawlers. That was not on the plan, to be surrounded by those one night. Not any night.

As he walked, the noise of the boy, the prisoner grew quieter. Faintly he heard the prisoner call out, but Darius did not turn back. He did not listen. He tried very hard not to care.

The Crawlers

The Crawlers. He could see them, eyes shining as they burrowed through the sand, mouths working, their hands sending up cartwheels of dust, their faces a festering of hunger. They were coming for him.

He was standing in the sand in the dark with only his staff, hot sweat rolling down his back. They moved forward swiftly, silently. He could feel his heart beating out of his chest. He would not go down this way, not allow himself to be consumed by these monsters! With a growl he lifted his staff high, as he felt hot teeth fasten hungrily onto his thigh. Sharp pain flared. He had to focus. They would not bring him down.

"I will not die by your hands," he growled, bringing the staff down hard, hearing the sick crunch, feeling the next grasp his elbow. He turned, raising his staff again...

Darius woke, cold with sweat, breath rushing past his teeth in short pants. His teeth were clenched, his fists furled, his body ready to leap into action. He was dreaming. He must have been dreaming, he was on his back in the cabin, it was dark, it was quiet. He was dreaming.

But it was not quiet. The slow fade of a scream rolled out in the night, faintly. Far away but there, they were out there. Had hearing them made him dream of them? Lying there for a moment he listened, trying to calculate how far out they were. They did not normally hunt here but he did not want them to begin. Saints, was it that fool of a prisoner who had drawn them so close? He felt his teeth clenching, the rage rising again.

They would not come so close, and change their hunting grounds to include his spot in the desert. The staff was at the door, dark in the shadow. He considered the sharpened shards of rock, stowed safely in his pack, and cursed. He should have fashioned them to his staff, or made something similar. But he had preferred to keep them hidden. The Warden did not want you to have real weapons that could threaten them, his Guards, of course, but they held all the cards in this world anyway. No prisoner who wanted to live would attack the Warden.

But the Crawlers were unarmed, witless except in their one remaining function, to rip apart and feed. A staff was enough. Without a look back at Mister, Darius strode out, stifling the urge to shout a warrior cry. He was hunting.

Pausing, he looked out at the night sky. The air was silent again, with only a faint hum of the wind. He waited. They would call again. It took but a moment, before the scream began, rising and falling. It sounded like it was coming from near the mountains. That was a fair distance for the Crawlers, who seemed to like to be in a close proximity to the Mines if they could. A cold chill struck. That wasn't so far from here. But it was also near... Maire's place. What if the prisoner had found it? It was an easy walk from where he had left him...

Darius shut his eyes, teeth clenched. This was his doing. He should have frightened the prisoner more, or killed him. It was his weakness in walking away, and now he had to pay for it.

Or the Crawlers would be a mere breath away. There was only one thing he could do.

He set off, staff in his fist, ready. Keeping to the rocks, he moved carefully, listening. Nothing out there moved. The dark hugged the plains, expectant. The sky was clouded, shrouding the moon. Darius did not need it anyway.

He knew where he was, how many breaths it took to get to the outcrop of rocks. Too few, if the Crawlers were there. The sand gleamed against the dark rock. It was too quiet. Darius paused, listening for movement. Or for signs of life in the shelter, if the boy had found it, Saints curse him. Lifting his head, he sniffed the air. He could not smell blood or death.

But there was something out there, in the dark. Something waiting. He could feel it, even if he could not see it. Quickening his pace, he concentrated on breathing through his nose, letting his heart calm and slow. The Crawlers would be listening for fear. They thrived on it.

He was almost at the outcrop. He shifted closer to the rock, moving himself along, face always on the plains. Looking out for the enemy that he knew was there.

You can always feel the eyes, his commander had once said. Even when you can't see them, you can feel them.

He could feel them now.

He risked a quick look into the clearing, eyes narrowed, trying to discern what was in the shadows. The shelter was deserted, maybe... wait! No, there was a pack, strewn carelessly in the middle of the lean to.

He stifled the curse that tried to fall from his lips. He had led this boy here, and brought himself danger. He should have killed him then and there. His mercy was the reason he was out here now.

If the pack was here, then the boy must not be far. He surveyed the area again, searching it methodically, looking back at the plain between sweeps. There was still no movement but the dark had thickened, stilled. Even the night was waiting for bloodshed, it seemed.

At last he saw him, or something that could be him, a slumped shape to the far edge of the clearing. Darius peered, trying to work out if that was something, or nothing at all. He could not make it out. It was not much more than an inkblot, a lump that was out of place. But out of place it was. It had to be him. He began to walk, turning his back at last to the plain. He moved quickly. If they were watching, they would use this opportunity to hunt.

He was almost at the edge when he heard the movement, the skitter of legs behind him. He felt his limbs galvanise, his focus deepen. The urge to survive always sharpened that edge.

"Move!" he yelled to the prone body. "Fight, or we die!"

He turned back, eyes wide, looking out at the dark.

Death waited no longer. His eyes turned from left to right, watching for movement. There. He could see the shift in the sand, the hump and fall as they moved under the surface. To his right, another was moving. Two, then.

The figure had not moved at his feet. Darius kicked at him, swiftly, not looking away from the moving humps in the sand.

"Get up! Do you want to be eaten? Fight!"

The Crawrlers were close, now, moving towards each other, honing in on their target. Darius adjusted his stance, steadying himself, holding his staff in both hands. It would be so much easier if he had the weapons he carried once, back when he served. But now he had nothing but his fists and his staff. It would have to be enough. They were coming. His eyes stayed on that telltale ripple in the sand as they readied themselves to leap, to fly out upwards.

"Fight!"

The roar leapt out of his mouth, unbidden. He did not look back, his hands throwing the staff left to stun the Crawler still in the sand, feeling the impact rattle his bones.

Turning, he raised the other part of the staff, bracing himself for the leap. The creature leapt, mouth hanging open. Darius thought he heard a whisper of something, a hiss, maybe, but he ignored it. He had to kill these two.

If they returned to the Mines then the route would be permanently changed from now on, their new hunting grounds.

He got a whiff of its breath, hot and rotten, as he shoved the staff hard into its throat, feeling the soft skin yield, the creature collapsing to the sand. He turned his eyes back to the other Crawler. He had seconds till it was on him.

It was moving already, its hands clawing at the sand, eyes wide. Darius felt a wave of revulsion as he looked at the thing. How could it once have been a person? What did it do to become this? But he did not have time to pity.

He stepped forward, closer, driving the staff down, hearing the crunch, the give of bone as he crushed its face. The body of it curled up, spider-like, hands flexing, toes curling. He lifted the staff, throwing it down, hard, hitting bone, again, again.

He was breathing hard now.

The other Crawler was rising. But so was the prisoner at last, panting, white face bright in the night. The prisoner was shaking like a leaf, eyes wide with fear. Darius looked at him briefly. "Staff."

His own staff was ready in Darius's hand.

The Crawler was focused on him, mouth open, eyes spitting with hate. He would not surprise it twice. This would be a bloody fight.

It lunged, hands reaching. Darius feinted, fending it off, feeling the wood glance off its shoulder. He breathed out hard. His heartbeat raced, breath burning in his throat.

Movement flashed beside him. The prisoner was moving now, his staff oversized in his hands, but he was using it, hitting out at the creature that was thrashing in the sand.

Had the kid struck a blow? The staff went down again, hitting at its leg, making it flinch.

Darius took his staff in hand, lunging at the Crawler's back, shoving the end as hard as he could, over and over again. He felt the skin give, the bones crack.

The prisoner's staff followed suit, complementing his rhythm. Hit, hit, hit.

Darius could only hear his breathing, heavy, short. His nostrils were full of the tang of blood, hot, metal.

"I think... we killed it," he breathed, panting from the exertion. The prisoner stared down, his staff poised.

Darius reached his hand out. "Did you hear me? I think we killed it."

The prisoner wheeled, staff raised, his mouth gasping for breath. Darius stepped back.

"Hey, hey. I'm not here to hurt you. Stand down."

He lowered the staff, still breathing heavily.

Darius watched him. "Alright. You need to be careful. Don't let those things follow you. If they go back to the Mines they will tell the others where people are. Don't settle in one place too long."

He turned, wearied, his back cold with sweat. He wondered if he was getting too old for this, if the next encounter would be his last. Would he mind, really? He shut out the thought. It was time to go back to his own shelter.

"Wait!"

The prisoner's voice was shrill, a scream. He did not turn his head but he waited. "What?"

"Please don't leave me here," came the whisper. It was a tortured sound. Darius hardened himself to it.

"I am not responsible for you, kid. Woestynn does not look after the weak. Get strong or get dying. Those are your only choices. Don't follow me. If you bring Crawlers near this place again, I will kill you."

A sob reached his ears which he shrugged away. He did not look at the bodies in the sand as he walked away, back to his hut. The moon shone out from brooding clouds as he walked, watching from afar. Once he would have found comfort in the moon, long ago, far away. But that was another person, another time. He walked back, slowly, surrounding himself by the silence.

Kail

The Sun stalked the clouds quietly, almost as if it, too, had been shaken by the experience last night. The Crawlers had come so near. Darius watched the morning waken, his staff in hand, not having moved from his position outside the hut. Did he defend the place where he stayed? He dismissed the notion.

But did he defend the solitude, the haven for creatures like Mister? Maybe. He did not know if he wanted to think about it. He was watching for Crawlers. That's all that mattered. They were the threat, and he was protecting ... something. He shifted position, feeling life return painfully to his limbs. He would need to avoid that if he wanted to be able to move quickly. The Crawlers might not come now, but they might tonight. He must be vigilant.

For a moment he was faced with himself, but as the people he could have been, if he had not taken the roads he had. What had happened to the earnest soldier, the one who wanted to change the world, to protect it? He knew what had happened. But what could he have been if he had not made those choices?

He grasped the staff, eyes wet, as he watched the ghosts of his past step out in front of him.

One, embracing his mama, resplendent in uniform. Another, hands covered in soil, tending to a garden in a green planet somewhere. Another, surrounded by young people, laughing.

"Enough," he growled. They dissipated, vanishing uncertainly into the still cool morning air. The desert waited, bleak sand and endless dunes. "Enough!"

He was not that person. He was something else now. He had claimed the life he had, and now he had to pay for it.

It was morning. Time to collect ore. Stepping into the hut, he collected his pack, trying to ignore the quiet of the hut. The sameness of it. It would not become a sanctuary. Even if it felt like it, just today. He stepped back out, ignoring the ache in his limbs, in the fatigue. One run of ore collecting, and then he could be done. He could find more tomorrow. Sleep when he got back. It was enough.

He had a flash of a thought about the prisoner, of Maire's Place. Would Maire have wanted him to help the prisoner?

Darius shut the thought down faster than he could blink. It was not his problem. He didn't need that kind of worry.

He set out, not intending to go near Maire's Place at all. There were plenty of routes that were nowhere near. But they would go nearer the Crawlers and he didn't want to leave his scent near for another to follow. He could kill Crawlers, but he didn't want to make a habit of it. He followed his usual route, resolving to not follow the rocks for a change. He would strike out into the desert for a while. It was early enough. The Sun wouldn't bother him for a couple of hours.

The desert was quiet, the sand undisturbed. He was glad of it. Striding, he tried to regain his rhythm, his focus. These were his days. It wasn't fair that his routine was disrupted. But the prison wouldn't give him extra quarter for that, even if he were a good prisoner, they needed the ore for goodness knows what. It didn't matter what they wanted it for, really. They needed it, and prisoners like him provided it.

The Gap loomed up on his right, still in shadow. He paused, hating himself. He had to keep going! He had ore to collect. He had no time to check on creatures who shouldn't be there. He was beyond that. Damn them.

Despite himself he felt his feet turning, just to check if he was still alive. Yeah, right. If the kid was still alive, he wouldn't last past the next encounter. Intervening was more cruel than leaving him in peace to die. He knew that. He had seen it too many times.

But there was something about his face, his despair. He would take one look. He didn't have to help him or anything.

It was quiet. It always was, nowadays, with a hint of the shadows of Maire's laugh echoing in the distance.

He did not stop by his hut all that often but sometimes he had, to listen to his stories. Some were absolutely too far fetched to be true, but he enjoyed them anyway. It almost made him feel human again. Alive. But then he died, as they all did in Woestynn. It was a blessing for the old man. He had been there too long. He wondered when that blessing would be coming for him.

The shadowed grey smudge of the mine loomed with menace, so far away. He wanted to rail at it. It was far but never far enough. Would the Crawlers come again? There was no knowing. He stepped back into the clearing, feeling the tension in his feet, the memories of the place.

Had the kid gone? He turned, the clearing rising up before him. The shack was empty. Did he want it that way? Part of him did. He had no room left to look after people anymore. He was tired. But his feet lingered.

"Hey kid!"

His voice echoed in the emptiness. Flinching at it, he waited, leaning on his staff, counting the seconds, ready to leave. He wasn't here. He was gone, had found somewhere else to die. That was the end of it, the end of his responsibility.

He counted in his head to twenty, hating himself every second. Did he want him to show up? Did he want him to be dead? It didn't matter. He wasn't here. He reached twenty and turned away. His feet dragged. It was better if he was dead, really. The kid would never survive here. But his eyes scanned once more, just in case. He was a fool.

There he was, almost invisible against the sand, wrapped in a blanket, leaning against the wall. His eyes were empty, dull. His mouth was dry, cracked from the heat. Darius paused, calculating. He wouldn't last much longer.

Why wasn't he walking away? His feet began walking closer, slowly, even as he cursed his treacherous feet. Just leave! Don't get involved! He's dead anyway! But he moved closer, noting the blank expression, the lack of reaction. The boy wasn't dead but he was near to it. He got near enough and crouched down, waiting for him to respond. The boy moved his eyes, a dull flicker of something appeared for just a moment, then was gone.

"You'll die here if you don't keep moving, kid."

The kid did not respond, making the slightest shrug with his shoulder.

Darius sighed, wondering what to do. "What's your name, kid?"

That got his attention. He turned, slowly, his face open with surprise. He opened his mouth and gasped out a breath, as quiet as dried leaves. He licked his lips, wincing, and tried again. "Kail. I'm called... Kail."

"I'm Darius."

Kail nodded, his mouth working as if he wanted to speak again. Darius shook his head. "You need to drink. Do you have your hydration tablets? Dying of thirst is not the way to go, kid. It's going to be a tough death. At least drink a little."

Kail didn't move. Sighing again, Darius brought down his pack, fishing about to find a tab. He could spare one. He handed it over, feeling as if he was trying to feed a baby bird out on the reserve like when he was young. His mind conjured up the cool lake and the salt breeze, before he shut it down. This was not the time or place for dreams. The kid, Kail, reached out and took the tab gingerly, as if it would bite him.

"That's it. Put it on your tongue. It will work quickly. Trust me. You need to get your strength back up."

Kail did as he was told, pushing it into his mouth and then subsiding, looking away. That dead look was back in his eyes. Darius looked up at the sky, wondering how long he had been out there. "Lets get to the shelter. You need to be in the shade before it gets too hot. Can you make it yourself?"

Please make it yourself, he thought. Don't rely on me. But Kail nodded, heaving himself up carefully, looking like a collection of bones under the blanket. He really wasn't going to last long. Slowly they walked to the hut, crossing the open space in silence. Darius did not know what to say. He didn't know why he had done this, be a saviour. It wasn't him. Not any more.

They reached the hut and Darius settled himself against the wall, using his pack as a prop. His hand still smarted from the winds. He would need to treat it again, or see if he could buy an ointment from the guards. Kail curled up in the corner, looking even smaller, even younger. Darius felt a twinge of sympathy.

"How long did you get?"

There was a long pause. Darius looked out to the sky, waiting. It was a personal question. Most of the time it was easy to work out what someone had done based on the length of sentence, and prisoners did not always want to share that detail. Some lied, not that it mattered here. Most of the people in Woestynn were here for terrible crimes.

"Five years."

The reply came suddenly. Kail was still in a huddled position but was looking at him, eyes huge in his face. "I should have got longer. I killed one of my clients. He was one of the rough ones, and I thought he was going to kill me this time. I fought him off and he died. They said it was an accident so they didn't give me very long, but they sent me here."

"A client?"

"I was a flesh worker. It was paying for my sister's education. I don't know what she'll do now. I've made such a mess of everything." Kail bowed his head, thin shoulders shaking.

"Five years isn't so long, Kail. Why don't you buy your way into the prison, stay there, and apply for a transfer? They might send you somewhere nicer."

Kail shook his head. "I don't think I can go back there. I don't think I can be locked away again."

Darius laughed. "And this is better? Waiting to be eaten by the Crawlers or scorched by the winds?"

Kail didn't respond.

"Well it's your choice, kid. You live or die the way you want to. Woestynn can't take that. Not yet, anyway."

They sat there in silence, as the wind blew and the sand kicked up its shapes. The sun was riding in a cloudless orange sky. Darius wouldn't be going anywhere for a while. Kail hadn't moved, huddled there, head against the rough wood. Darius wondered how old he was, why he was selling his body to strangers. Why he was helping his sister and not his parents. But it wasn't his place to ask.

He opened his mouth to say something, offer food perhaps, anything to break the silence. Instead he started speaking about his own life.

"I think I have been here for a year. I was locked up awaiting trial for some time before being sent here. I was sentenced to three hundred years."

Kail was watching him, eyes like saucers. Darius laughed, a bitter laugh without humour. "Yes, lad, I did some bad things. I don't even have an excuse. I had a nice family, a career, a nice home. I didn't have to get into the things I did, but I did. And now I have to pay for the blood on my hands. I won't ever leave Woestynn, not ever. The prison guards won't be shipping my body home in a box. I said goodbye to my family before my trial and told them to forget me. I won't see them again. I probably don't deserve to. But I won't pay my way into that prison either. If my only choices are to die in a cell or die out here, I'll take my chances out here. At least I can die on my own feet, on my own terms. So that's why I am here."

"And do you want to?"

Darius didn't bother to ask him what he meant. Every prisoner wanted to die, to some extent. "Yes," he replied somberly. "Although when I think death is staring me in the face, I am afraid. Some part of me doesn't want to give up yet. It wants to live for something."

Kail shifted, wincing again. "I don't. I'm not afraid. I don't have anything left to live for."

There was nothing else to say. Darius sat next to the boy, thinking, and at last Kail settled into a fretful, troubled sleep.

The Cliff People

Darius shivered in the cold morning light, wishing he had brought his extra scarf. He had started out for the dunes long before daybreak, looking out warily in the dark. But it was quiet and no animal or demon disturbed his journey. It had been easier going without his pack, but he had brought his staff and a makeshift blade just in case.

Nothing stirred. The road that he had spotted last time was empty. This time he went straight to the edge, looking down. He could feel no vibrations in the earth, hear no sounds. It was as if everything had been paused, placed into hibernation. Darius looked around, wondering where he could climb down to the bottom. There did not seem to be any ladders or ropes to the valley below, and the drop was sheer.

But Pilgrim had appeared from somewhere. And this time he was going to find him.

He turned to his left, following the edge carefully. The sand was soft, interspersed with small stones. Slowly, the land sloped downward, a gentle sweep towards the valley below. He continued, listening for signs of movement. Surely there would be people, movement, noise. Where did they come from? Where did they live? His feet found a trail of sorts, and turned to follow it. It zigzagged down the hill, sliding past a few spiky, bare shrubs that clung to the hillside.

Fear warred with something else, something that he hadn't felt for a while. Anticipation. Was he really going to throw his lot in with Pilgrim? Being around other people, after so long, scared him. The wind whispered through the sparse shrubs and he listened warily. It sounded like the normal wind. He walked on, using his staff to steady him on the loose ground. The still weak sun rose, casting long shadows through the sand. The trail levelled out, turning to hug the slope, and at last he could see more of the underside of the cliff and the strange valley.

His eyes widened as he realised that the area was not empty at all. Nestled into the cliff were makeshift shelters, camouflaged with coloured fabric, branches and stone. People lived here, inside the cliff. His eyes swept over the cliff again, looking for the dark spots that he had thought were entrances. There were two, tall archways leading into a dark tunnel. One was wide enough for a vehicle to use and the sand was flattened, as if something heavy had stamped the ground into submission. Warily, he walked towards the other archway, adjusting the grip on his staff and reassuring himself that his makeshift blade was in place. He might need it.

Thoughts whirled in his mind. This could be an entire community, under the cliff. How far in did the tunnels go? It must be a relief to step into the cool, away from the sun. It could almost make the place bearable. The archway was narrower than the other, lined in grey brick. He could see nothing at the other end, and hear nothing. It couldn't be deserted. Pilgrim had mentioned a group.

He stepped into the archway, feeling the tiny stones shift underfoot. The ground of the passageway must be something solid, stone, perhaps. Was this connected to the mines? A cold finger of fear touched the back of his neck and he shivered. No, the mines were far away, unless the network was across the entire planet. And there could have been collapses deep underground. No, this must be separate.

It was cooler already, in the shade, and his eyes welcomed it. He walked, eyes darting from right to left, looking for disguised passageways or people lying in wait. There were one or two alcoves set into the wall but they were empty. He looked forward, seeing a slight lift in the gloom. There was no light, that he could see, but the passageway was about to open up into something. He stepped forward carefully, intent on making no noise. He reached the edge of the passage, holding the edge of the smooth wall for balance.

The passage opened out into a great underground cavern, dimly lit with bioluminescent plants that clung to the walls. The soft green light was eerie, too weak to cast shadows, but the cast of it made the cavern look as if it was underwater perhaps, or on an entirely different planet. He stared and stared, seeing in front of him a great circular complex, set into a ring of steel walkways that ran around the edges. Clever, he thought. People who came in to attack would be funnelled through the passageways and it would be easy to pick them off.

There was little movement that he could see. There were a few figures in dark clothing at the far end of the cavern, but the part nearest to him seemed to be quiet, uninhabited. He wondered what made the clanging, rhythmic noise that he had heard. He wondered how he would find Pilgrim in this vast place. He felt overwhelmed by it, by the sheer scale of the settlement. Somehow, these people had created a functioning society entirely underground.

There was no way but down, or to stay on the walkway flanking the perimeter. Which was more likely to bring him to the man he sought?

He weighed his options, eyeing the tunnel behind him and the bustle of movement below. There were steps nearby, leading down into the main area, so he climbed down, eyes on the walkway above. He would be ready if someone saw him. Keeping to the shadows, he moved past a cluster of tents, seeing more passageways leading to the rock on the other side. The cavern layout was more intricate than he had realised, looking like a honeycomb with a myriad of passages leading further into the rock.

He avoided them, keeping to the main walls of the cavern, eyes on the people moving about at the far end. Nobody had seemed to notice him yet, or did not care about his presence. The cavern grew a little lighter, causing Pilgrim to look up in surprise. Small shafts of light filtered down from cracks in the rock above. It was narrow enough to not bring in the heat and searing bright of the sun, but enough to brighten the cavern. He looked behind him, making sure nobody was following him. There was nothing else to do but approach the people and hope that they knew the person he was looking for. There were a group of three in quiet discussion, heads bent together. He walked towards them, head held high, stride wide. As he walked they turned towards him, faces curious.

"Greetings, friends. I seek Pilgrim. Do you know him?"

One, a tall man with an intricate plait sprouting from the back of his head, curved an elegant eyebrow.

His skin was darker, eyes gleaming in an intelligent face.

"And why do you want Pilgrim?"

"I met with him some days ago. He said that I could visit his community."

The tall man did not react, eyes assessing steadily. "Did he give you anything?"

"A copper disc."

The men relaxed slightly, smiles growing on their faces. Plait man put his hand out.

Darius fished into his coat, fingers closing on the small piece of metal. He presented it, but did not hand it over. The man's eyes narrowed.

"I was told to present it, but I have not yet made my decision. I was hoping to speak again with Pilgrim first."

Plait nodded imperceptibly to another, who hurried off. The other, a man with no hair and bright green eyes, stepped closer, extending his hand.

"I'm Zet. I've not been here that long. Good to meet you, friend."

Darius responded to the gesture awkwardly. "Darius."

Plait Man did not move to shake hands. "Dree. Greetings, Darius."

The third man returned, the tall figure of Pilgrim beside him. His hair was as wild as the last time he had seen him, but this time he was not wearing a jacket. He smiled toothily, looking more like a wolf than a man. Darius forced himself to smile back. "Friend, it is nice to see you again. I confess, I did not expect to see you so soon. Normally people take longer before they come to find me again. Are you ready to join us?"

Darius hesitated. Pilgrim smiled again, his eyes taking in the scene. "Come and walk with me, Darius. I'll show you around."

He nodded to the men, who nodded back, walking away.

"So, what can I do for you, Friend?"

He gestured towards one of the wider passageways, strolling towards it. Darius strode to catch up, watching the easy grace of Pilgrim. This man was in good health. Strong, too. "I came across a new prisoner, a young one, called Kail. He has been sentenced to five years, but he doesn't want to go into the prison."

Pilgrim snorted. "I doubt we can blame him, friend. I wouldn't either. So," he paused, looking at Darius. "Why isn't he here?"

"He's not in very good shape. He wants to take his own life."

A flicker of sadness crossed Pilgrim's wizened face. "And you're hoping he finds something better here. Is he weak?"

"Very."

"Hmm. Hmm." Pilgrim walked along in deep thought, one hand in his pocket. Darius walked beside him, eyeing the smooth walls of the tunnel, the pale green light of the plants. They passed a small group of people who appeared to be working on the wall foundations, perhaps.

"We are a small community, friend, but we all must pay our way. Everyone has to work and contribute. If your friend cannot, then someone must pay towards his board, you understand me?"

Darius understood him. "I can stand as surety for him."

Pilgrim studied him for a moment. "Well then I think we have a deal. If you come, then he can come too. I think you will do mighty well in my team, Darius. You have a brain. And I am sure we can fit your friend in somewhere."

He stopped, putting out his hand to shake. "I'll be seeing you, then?"

Darius shook his hand, acknowledging the dismissal. "Thank you, Pilgrim."

Pilgrim put his hand to his head as if he was touching an invisible hat. "Oh, thank you, Darius. I think you are going to be quite the asset."

He chuckled as he turned, beginning to whistle an unfamiliar tune, striding off down the passageway. Darius watched him for a moment before turning back towards the cavern, to start the long walk back over the dunes.

No more waiting

His hand found the disc in his pocket. He kept doing that, lately, to make sure it was there. He kept thinking of the community under the rock, the future he could have if he wanted it. Did he want that? What if he could get in touch with his family? Would he break his promise of silence and contact them? He did not know.

He walked towards Maire's Place, spirits light. Perhaps Kail would listen, and take some food and water, attempt the walk to the mountain community. Perhaps he would flourish there, and find some purpose. Darius felt hopeful. He felt light.

Approaching the hut, he called out to Kail, seeing him curled up against the wall of the hut. He looked peaceful.

"Kail. I've got news."

Kail didn't stir, his eyes closed. Darius drew closer, crouching down, hand pulling out another hydration tab to offer the boy. He put his other hand out to touch him, carefully. He paused.

"Kail. Speak to me." Even as he spoke his heart grieved. He wouldn't speak again. He could see the pallor now, the waxy sheen of death in the boy's face. He had died. He died alone, in this place. Darius sat down heavily next to him.

"I found you a place to go, Kail. You could have got strong and well. But perhaps this is better. I hope you find peace, kid."

Pulling himself to his feet, he took his staff, looking for a last time at Maire's hut, at the memories of it. He did not look back again. It was a short distance to walk to his hut, to pick up his pack, to bury his extra supply of food and hydration tablets, next to the pack of tea. He might need to have that."

The sun was dying away, a wrinkled blob on the horizon, as he shut the door to his hut, the home he had built in this desert. Mister perched on his shoulder, looking out on the desert sea. Darius held the disc in his hand, thinking.

There would be no more waiting. No more waiting to die.

He strode out, holding his staff, away from the hut, away from his ghosts. He did not look back.

About the Author

Eryn was born and raised in Oxford, UK but nowadays lives in South Germany with their young family. They want to travel the world and visit all the mountains, lakes and of course vineyards. When they are not dreaming of travel or writing poetry, they work as a freelance English teacher.

Eryn is a poet and an accidental novelist. They studied Poetry and Playwriting at University but never actually intended to write fiction at all. That changed sometime in 2021 when they began to write flash fiction, which then grew into short stories, and then a couple of those stories developed into ideas for a novel.

Their writing largely leans to the dystopian and the idea that all characters are morally grey. The Woestynn series are about that concept, that each and every person is equally bad and equally good. Does doing bad things mean you are a bad person? What if you believe it to be right?

Eryn is currently working on the remainder of the Woestynn series, the next books in the Sovereign series, and is considering a return to the Ruben system, but in something decidedly more cheerful.

Eryn is at present obsessed with cheese, dragons, brown noise and strange esoteric videos on Youtube that combine rain noises with desert storms and tombs. When not writing you can find them on Twitter, generally spreading upheaval of some kind or another.

Milton Keynes UK
Ingram Content Group UK Ltd.
UKHW011812190923
428965UK00004B/380